THE NAVIGATOR WHO CROSSED THE ICE WALLS

WORLDS BEYOND THE ANTARCTICA

NOS CONFUNDEN

CLAUDIO NOCELLI

CONTENIDO

THE NAVIGATOR WHO CROSSED THE ICE WALLS

WORLDS BEYOND THE ANTARCTICA

NOS CONFUNDEN

THE NAVIGATOR WHO CROSSED THE ICE WALLS: WORLDS BEYOND THE ANTARCTICA

- "TERRA-INFINITA MAP" -

CHAPTER I – TO ANTARCTICA

My name is William Morris, and the story that you are about to read, It is probably going to modify the current way of seeing the world, I know most of people will find it incredible and believe me, even having experienced this adventure, having seen it with my own eyes and with all my senses, it was also incredible to myself, but the evidence is irrefutable for those who want to see it and the memories indelible, such evidence will be presented and science will also change its perspective, another path will be opened in the human mind forever.

 As for my personal life, I was a member of the Continental Navy, as the American naval force was called in the Revolutionary War, I was married to Lucy and we were thinking of enlarging the family, but the war postponed every plan, as it usually does, with that pain that probably feel cutting the root of that shining tree that gives life to the garden, that immense pain that produces to move away from your loved ones and go to hell itself.

One peaceful night after the surrender of Saratoga, we were sailing through the northern Atlantic Ocean, rounding the islands on our way to Charleston Harbor, the full moon was the only light that illuminated our way and during that night, thousands of stories and anecdotes arose among the boys over a little whiskey to calm the anxieties of a raw war.

Even then, there was talk of James Cook's voyages and his obsession with crossing the "Antarctic Circle", although it was not clear who was behind his funding or why the obsession, as I was not well steeped in the subject the talk had not captivated me enough, I did not pay much attention and the boys went on with the stories.

Captain Butler, well respected in the group, joined in the sailing stories by commenting that it was possible that there was a passage somewhere in the Polar Circle, and that this passage could be the connector to other worlds, he said it seriously without a moment's hesitation.

My attention turned to him, and the five or six of us in that cabin were speechless listening to his story, we expected him to say that it was a joke but that never happened, we could not believe that a captain was seriously telling that there could be lands behind the Antarctic Circle.

Butler commented that he knew from good sources at the highest levels that they were researching and funding voyages to penetrate the harsh climate and barriers in the southern latitudes to find possible land and perhaps civilization beyond the Antarctic continent, and that they were in a hurry to carry out these missions as many civilian navigators were circling the area and did not look favorably on anyone else coming along.

This story was even longer and in great detail, he also commented that he observed with his own eyes a map that indicated the coordinates that could be the opening of such a passage, and although he was stupefied by this story and I think the others too, the fatigue and stress generated by a war conflict could not be wasted, it was the perfect moment of happiness that generates a breach of peace to be able to sleep a few hours.

Time went by and after the famous war, many of the ships used by the Continental Navy were rented, destroyed, captured or sold, as at that time I was a person of good economic standing, especially after a war that we could say "triumphant" (if after a war can be called so) I made an offer for one of them and managed to keep it, although my colleagues always scoffed at me because of that, as they say it was ridiculously high for such an old ship.

The idea of the exploration trip to the south, after Butler's story, generated even more interest for me to bid and keep the ship, although it needed repairs (therefore some extra money) I felt no guilt as I felt it as an investment, although I did not know the real danger of such a trip, I needed to provide myself with a great navigation equipment.

Although Lucy was not happy about this plan, I was planning to leave Charleston by the end of November and head, with a few stops along the way, straight to the Antarctic continent.

During the idea of forming the team, I talked to former colleagues, some of them made the most ridiculous excuses, and I don't blame them either, the idea of such a trip was really not encouraging, two of them, who were there that same night that Butler told his story, wanted to join as soon as I told them about the plan, But the most difficult part was to convince Butler, who had knowledge in navigation based on his experience and leadership, and also knew the coordinates where we should go, after gathering courage for a few weeks, I contacted the captain to tell him about my project and add him to the group.

It was difficult to convince the captain of such a plan, and although in his voice I noticed some enthusiasm, he declined my offer, and it was like that for a while.

Unexpectedly on the morning of October 11th he showed up at my home with another companion named "Fint", he had maps that I had never seen and was full of documents that very few eyes had read, he told me that he accepted the deal but that he was willing to understand that it could only be a one way trip, then I understood that we had to take this trip professionally, the adventure was about to begin.

CHAPTER II - THE CUSTODIANS

After such a phrase from the captain, we finalized details and agreed on a departure date, it would be November 14th, his mysterious partner Fint, as he introduced himself, would also join the team, my boat would be ready even a month before.

Those were days of much anxiety and little sleep, a lot of reading and meetings with the team about the trip we were planning, we fantasized about the most incredible adventures but reality was about to surpass any possible fiction or imagination.

On November 12th, just two days before leaving, Fint (Butler's partner) showed up at my door with another man who looked even more mysterious than him, all dressed in black and with a strange accent, he told me it was urgent and I made them enter my home.

Fint had a briefcase which he opened as soon as he entered on top of a table, inside there were many documents and among them he took out a kind of ancient manuscript, and began to recite a part of it:

"Then by demand, I subscribe in major importance, here by desire of our lords that the doors of knowledge be closed to those who refused to be part of our glorious path and liberties granted", the text went on for several more lines and then at the end the so called "Poem Regius" was recited.

As soon as he finished his reading, I commented that it seemed that he was in some kind of initiation rite, it was then when Fint commented:

- Exactly comrade, precisely those who did not pass this initiation, are the marginalized, better said, we are the marginalized.

Fint, I demanded, please explain a little, I am not understanding anything, what does this text mean and what does it have to do with our trip?

- Look, Fint commented, I am going to explain a little of the situation, this manuscript belongs to "The Custodians" as we call them, or as they call themselves "The Sun-Gods" and they found out about your trip through Butler, the high spheres are aware of it and it does not make them happy, this manuscript raises that they will not let anyone leave these lands by demand of the Lords.
The situation could not get any worse, an adventure that was already risky enough due to the harsh weather and everything that could happen to us due to natural events, now we were adding these unknown enemies.

Who are these "Custodians"? I asked.

Fint went around in circles, and his strange friend opened his mouth for the first time, interrupting, he commented that these Custodians were not happy about our trip and that was the only thing they could tell me.

Fint then suggested that We should cancel it, that it wasn't worth risking our lives, he said it with a threatening tone, that's when I then invited them to leave my house immediately.

His strange friend looked at me defiantly and they left, after a few minutes I tried to communicate with Butler to ask him what was happening and comment on the situation of this strange visit, Butler never answered, neither that day nor the following ones, I gathered the emergency team to analyze how to continue, this travel plan was becoming dark and sinister, but an inner force pushed me to continue, the passage to other lands was becoming even more real but also more dangerous.

We met with the whole team, Butler was not there, nobody knew about him for weeks, he was missing, I told them the whole sequence about the visit of Fint and his partner, also about the Manuscript, Walter said he had heard something about "The Custodians" but he was not sure who they really were or if it was a secret organization.

The situation was not at all encouraging, Butler did not show up and the plan without him seemed impossible to carry out, besides the risk it seemed to entail against an unknown organization that was chasing us without even having left port.

We made the decision to postpone the trip again until we could find Butler, we would try again to find him at his home the next day.

As expected, we were unable to find Butler, and the chances of the trip were being destroyed by the minute along with the concern of the captain's whereabouts, the team also communicated with other known people and members of the naval force, nobody knew anything about him, it seemed as if he had been swallowed by the earth.

November 14th arrived, with the plan already cancelled, someone knocked on my door and to my total surprise, it was Captain Butler with provisions, maps and everything necessary to leave, he commented to me as if it was nothing, "It is time to leave, comrade".

I asked him as many times as possible where he had gone, and I also had to explain to him the strange last two days that the whole team had spent, he looked at me very coldly and commented "it was to be expected, I had to hide for security and priority to protect the documents needed for the plan", especially this "map" while I was unfolding it on the table in my living room, it was huge.

There was land I had never seen before, Butler ordered me to assemble the team and that we had to leave today.

I asked him if he knew "The Custodians" and he told me that there was a lot he had to tell, "the story is not the one we were told, William" "the creators of the Pyramids and another race, as they also call them "Custodians", have no interest in us crossing the South Pole", he told me that they found out about our travel plan via Fint, who had betrayed him, and that the trip had to be made today or we would never be able to make it, he also commented that we would have plenty of time later on to give me more details about all this once we are sailing.

I hurried to gather the whole team, once we were all together, we left the port of Charleston, we had a few stops before reaching the frozen areas of the South.

CHAPTER III - WE HAVE CROSSED THE WALLS

We set sail at last from Charleston harbor, Captain Butler was leading this adventure that we calculated between a few stops to arrive with enough provisions, we would be reaching the cold Antarctic waters in about 140 to 150 days at the most.

As we left we all had a mixture of excitement and panic from everything we had experienced in the previous days, we were also not quite sure why Butler had hidden himself in this way, had we become the enemies of a force we were going to be able to actually face? Butler also mentioned "another race" what had we really gotten ourselves into.

The days went by and everything was going very well, we had plenty of provisions and the companions were encouraging each other, beyond some sporadic storms the ship withstood the winds very well, when crossing the Equator we made some stops and stocked up again on the advice of the captain, who told us that the trip was going to be longer than we expected in the case of being able to cross the South Pole, We were also able to bring some cases of bottles of alcohol, although the heat of the tropic at that time did not let us think clearly, it was known that times of darkness and cold in the black waters of the south were approaching.

The second night of leaving the last port straight to Antarctica, I was on deck looking at the horizon and thinking about this adventure, the memories came all together to my mind, everything I left behind and if this turning against someone powerful was really worth it, I had an inner fire of curiosity, to know about this passage, if it was really possible to cross it, I wondered what would be behind, while all this was going through my mind Butler approached.

- Already cold, comrade? You can't imagine what awaits you then, he asked me.

- So you've been there? - I asked again

- Where do you mean, in the southern waters?, yes of course, Butler affirmed.

- That story you were telling that night, was it about you?

- I was there William, I saw that passage with my own eyes, that's why I'm wanted;

All doubt left my mind, the captain then gave a clear version about his past voyage, the lights went on in me and illuminated all curiosity, I couldn't wait to fill him with questions, but he stopped me right there almost as if reading my mind.

Then he told me, don't worry William, you will see it too, you will see what I saw with my eyes and you won't believe it either, and I'm not just talking about the passage, but I won't talk about it until we can get there.

The captain closed the conversation at the best moment, I had as many questions as the reader will have at this moment and I assure you that they will be answered in due time, the intrigue ate me inside and my face was the same tone as the reddish sun that began to appear on the horizon.

At one hundred and thirty eight days we were in the icy waters and the sudden difference was abysmal, the water was dark and as dark as the waves that swung us from one side to the other, the storm that had been chasing us for eight days was getting worse, the captain was calm and that gave us some security, but every time a wave crashed against our boat in our minds we could not not remember the warm home we were leaving behind, but I was confident in this mission, I knew somehow that it was going to give us its fruit.

We crossed a huge mountain that we had as a reference, where warm and cold winds intermingled even under the snow, as strange as the waters we were sailing, it is very difficult to describe this place, it is simply unique, it has a beauty that enamors even being aware that a second is enough to end your life against the huge masses of ice floating around.

We were now sailing parallel to a giant wall of ice that loomed, we calculated that it would be between 80 and 90 meters high, and in some places there were peaks of even more height but it was impossible to see it, the sleet could be seen up to a certain height, what we noticed and called our attention (except the captain who had already experienced it) is that reddish and yellow color that sometimes appears on the horizon, as if a ravenous fire of some forest was raging behind.

Near this giant mountain, blocks of ice fell like absorbent cotton on a mattress of snow forming a steep slope where the snow water melted and cascaded into the sea, an imposing image with this kind of reflection of fire behind, if this were portrayed in a painting, they would pay millions to have it, this view overwhelmed with a unique beauty and a sepulchral silence accompanying the lonely boat that the team decided to name "The Secret".

The weather was inhospitable, it did not give us any respite, the fight was daily against the waves and the wind, the danger of collision against the great masses of ice and the water that fell on us like an eternal cry from the sky, we decided then to approach again to the enormous Mount, The strange heat emanating from the melting ice all around gave the strange appearance that it did not fit, that it should not be there, but it even seemed to generate a different climate, we decided with the captain to skirt it as much as possible and investigate thoroughly this strange portion in front of the giant ice barriers.

Butler shouted my name and called me on deck, a passage opened up behind between the giant frozen walls, the happiness that enveloped us was unexplainable, but we knew that we would not be there for a long time.

Butler did not hesitate for a second and we were all stunned, the ship was heading that way, the captain seemed to know what he was doing and left the boat parallel to the promontory, and then a kind of current took us inside without even thinking twice, we were dragged by an enormous force, fear paralyzed us, we brushed the edges of that wall several times, all this panic lasted three or four minutes but inside us it seemed to be eternal.

Suddenly and once we were sailing on this current that was dragging us, calm seemed to invade our surroundings, the storm ceased and although the cold was still lashing it was no longer overwhelming, we were in an inexplicable ecstasy, this narrow passage was opening more and more and gave way to an open sea, my eyes did not lie although I doubted them several times.

The captain shouted, "We made it! We made it! And we all celebrated with surprise and amazement, we were in waters that only very few reached, or so we thought at that moment at least.

The dark waters began to clear, the ice walls were still visible but were being lost in the distance, the sun that contemplated our feat was falling on the horizon, it was time to boast.

I gathered the team by decision of the captain, who called us all with some seriousness, he was going to make an important announcement, he began by saying that what he was going to comment was not about him, nor about the team, nor about the known Earth we were leaving behind, it was about the whole of humanity and its past.

CHAPTER IV - THE WAR BEHIND THE WALLS

When we were all in silence waiting for the words of the captain, who was going to tell us something that seemed to be unique, a colossal sized craft loomed and seemed to be coming straight at us, one of the boys went up to see what he could spot and shouted as he descended in a violent manner, "They are coming towards us", "it is something gigantic".

We all panicked but Butler ordered to remain calm, although he remained calm, he seemed a bit nervous compared to what we had been experiencing before, this made me more uneasy, who would be coming towards us in this giant craft?

As it got closer, we did not change the north course, it had a reddish color and as it got closer we could see that it was more and more immense, I will not deny that I feared for my life and that of the team, I could not believe that we had just left the walls of ice behind, something was going to prevent us from continuing to investigate this unknown ocean, I also thought that we were the only ones who had come so far in these areas, we did not know exactly the depth but the ocean still looked dark.

A deafening sound enveloped us we could hardly stand it, it was a screeching sound like some kind of horn, then a voice with a perfect English accent came before us, saying the following;

"Dear visitors from the walled lands, some of our men will come down and approach your boat, we will do you no harm, please remain calm.

calm."

This message sounded even more frightening, inside me I thought they might attack us but it's not like we could escape from there either, this ship was gigantic and looked like something out of a fictional tale from a far future, Butler reassured us by acknowledging that he was aware that something like this could happen, to stay calm and welcome this new visitor in a kind way.

Three men were making their way to our ship, this was the first time we had ever had a visitor and we were not even sailing in familiar waters nor were any familiar people coming aboard, the men had white suits and some emblems stood out on them, there was a flag flying on top of their ship, if we could call it that, said flag was completely blue with a white circle in the center.

We helped the men up and they greeted us kindly by shaking our hands.

One of them introduced himself as the captain and asked us what we were doing sailing in this area across the wall.

Butler spoke for us and informed him that we were sailing around the Antarctic Arctic Circle and that a current had brought us to "the other side", and that we had decided to sail through these areas to investigate it, it would be my impression at the time but I had noticed a certain camaraderie between Butler and the officers.

The same man turned to look at his other two companions and they were amazed at such a feat, they commented among themselves that it had been a long time since they had seen something like this,

he apologized for the way they should have approached us and also the way they had to approach, saying the following words he explained to us the reason for this concern;

"We are very sorry that your visit does not seem to be welcome, it really is, but it has been a long time since we have seen people crossing the walls, in fact we do not know how they left them either... but it does not matter now, I will give you this map with directions on how to get to safe lands."

This last sentence was not well taken by any of the group, we looked at each other with some fear, I encouraged myself to ask then "safe lands did you say? are there then unsafe lands?".

"Well, the lands where you come from are quite unsafe" replied the man standing behind, "don't worry, you will get there fine sailing in this direction".

It was a unique moment to be able to understand the situation a little, I spoke again as the owner of the boat, "Excuse me, where do you come from?", I had millions of questions in my head.

From "The Ancestral Republic", sir, - the man answered me in a bounded way, adding later "don't worry, I understand that you have many questions at this

I promise you that they will give you all the necessary information when they arrive to these lands that we indicated to you, we will inform you that they will arrive so you can receive them immediately".

The men withdrew quickly, looking in all directions as if searching for something, the strange visit left us with more questions than answers, Butler did not hesitate for a moment and as a great leader, he woke up the group that was still fearful and somewhat hesitant, the destination was clear now, we were heading to new lands called "The Ancestral Republic".

We sailed for quite a while following the course indicated by these men, Butler indicated that it was important to follow this direction rigorously, when several of us from the team asked the captain about what he was going to tell us before the visit, he preferred not to continue with the subject, as if he had changed his mind outright, although he told us the following,

"After what happened I think we all have to open our eyes, fortunately we ran into these people and we can

We ran into these people and we can head to safe lands, I think we would not have had the same luck if it was another boat that visited us, let's remember that there are people we left behind, very powerful people who do not want us to be sailing these waters, or knowing all this, let's wait to arrive as soon as possible to The Republic and then they will understand more about the situation, it is something complex, but I am glad we have crossed the walls, the journey has just begun comrades, it is time to understand that we are in a war zone, doing something unique".

The last sentence left us speechless, we all asked in unison, "What do you mean, in a war zone?

War zone, what kind of war, what kind of war, what kind of war?" all the questions were directed to the captain, who answered them all by saying, "comrades, pay attention and let's get to these lands indicated, everything will become clear as soon as we anchor".

The temperature had changed quite a bit as we moved away from the walls, in about 30 days the area enveloped us with a temperate climate, as indicated we would be close to these lands, birds of various types began to be spotted, and vegetation on the waters that were now clearer, I had an inner feeling that we were making history forgetting a little the captain's phrase that we were in War zone without knowing it, in that case I would like to know, who was the enemy.

CHAPTER V - THE HUMAN RESET

On a clear night we could see in the distance, different lights that went from east to west illuminating the way and our hopes in a mild but very dark night, Butler observed the group that was stupefied by such beauty, it was a giant and silent city, it seemed an electric world out of a book by Thomas Browne.

We decided not to wait any longer in unknown waters because of the possibility of being attacked by an enemy that we still did not know because of the warning of the ship that had intercepted us when we crossed the walls and alerted us about the danger and about this supposed war that was being fought, although we were supposed to have arrived to safe lands, nothing seemed safe at that time.

We arrived at the port of what looked like a large and modern City, we were on deck waiting to be received, in less than two minutes several agents dressed in similar Uniform that those on that ship were wearing approached us, and in a very respectful way they welcomed us;

- "Welcome to the Ancestral Republic", one of them pronounced while shaking hands with Butler.

- "We are happy of your visit to our Lands, it was something unthinkable, we were informed that you would come but anyway we could not believe it until we saw it with our eyes, your visit is so rare not to say impossible, but here is our joy to receive you" - he pronounced.

Butler thanked on behalf of the whole boat, and introduced me as the owner of the boat, I was going through all the emotions together that can be imagined and immediately wanted my questions to be answered, although the fear of being in unknown lands in many occasions overcame the strong emotion of having discovered something immense, I was carried away by the latter, I think the whole team started with the idea that this trip had every chance of going wrong, but here we were in the land behind Antarctica and being welcomed by citizens of a modern city, it was time to ask everything.

It is an honor to visit these lands that until today were unknown to us, I proclaimed.

Before I mentioned anything else, this agent interrupted me saying that he had to take me to the Office of the President of the Republic himself, since our visit was almost unprecedented, that furthermore the President was aware of it and had notified that we take him immediately with him. He asked me to accompany him and looking at Butler who nodded his head, I went after him among some people who observed the situation, we were strangers who came from inhospitable lands, I think this generated such confusion in people as in ourselves.

A vehicle that I had never seen in all my life was waiting for us, there was not even a corner, at least in this part of the City, that was not reached by the illumination by the great lanterns that adorned and generated the sensation of being in a tale of the best writers.

The silence of the City was now more understandable knowing that there were no carriages, horses, or any type of vehicle that I knew from my experience in big cities like New York, the difference was abysmal in everything, their clothes were also colorful, the agent that accompanied me had in his hands a luminous device that transmitted different images and voices, the language that was spoken was different and I did not understand a single word.

A huge stone building stood out among the rest, with large and clear letters it said "Presidential Office Rebirth" and the flag of his country was highlighted by a perfect illumination, the blue circle in the center seemed to stand out.

When we arrived I followed the agent until we entered this immense building, there were connections for the passage between each room, there were seats of different types, the lighting was dim, when passing to one of those rooms I touched one of the walls, which were as cold as marble, I had again some fear about everything I was living, I understood the protocol that our visit was not common but I was already dizzy between so many stairs we climbed.

The agent asked me to wait for him in one of the comforting seats, the truth is that I could have waited there for hours, the comfort of those were indescribable, a tall man with a mustache came out to greet me:

- "So you are William Morris from the United States of America?" - he asked. That's right, I answered

This gentleman shook me tightly by the hand, commenting that he was sorry to receive me in one of the worst situations experienced in that Republic, in fact he commented as follows:

- "My name is Fhael, I am sorry that you have arrived in these times we are going through, it would have been totally different your visit and our reception in normal situations, you will know how to understand now when I put it in context."

I had so much confusion and questions that I could not say a single word.

- You see Mr. Morris, the situation is extreme and there are moments of tension, this war was usually seen from afar and now we are part of it, I should explain many points for you to understand, but I will have to be limited because I have many men sailing at this time and they need valuable information.

I nodded my head as if pretending to understand everything, only to give way to the story, hence some answers that could place me in situation.

- "Maybe you don't fully understand it yet, but we are part of what we could call "the old humanity", I mean, we were not part of the last reboot process, do you understand me?"

I would have every desire to be able to say that I understand but the truth is that I am lost in all this, what do you refer to as ancient humanity? How many humanities exist or existed?

- "There were many humanities in different times, as well as there were many resets or reboots, this happens every certain time already stipulated or it is done before that date for external reasons, I mean in a way intentionally created before reaching that time, as far as we know here in reality it always happens this way since the "natural" way is also carried out by the same by manipulating the environment where you come from."

What is this "human reset"?

- "The reboot is a process they carry out in their lands to annihilate every human being leaving only their newborn babies to repopulate those lands and carry out the same process over and over again, the reasons for the reboot according to our information is carried out when something gets out of the control of those who rule on the other side of the Ice Walls, the factors can be several and they do not doubt it, believe me, the knowledge of other lands can lead to a reset, it could be by pests, floods, fires, plagues, wars, missiles or war bombs they call asteroids, or it could be all that together, it doesn't matter how, the fact that we have escaped before is reason enough of a threat for them not to want us breathing, do you understand me now William? "

My head was spinning, I felt dizzy and thought I would fall there in front of this Mr. Fhael, while I understood the situation I could not believe that all that was happening in the lands where I was born, I sat up in a hurry and started to sweat cold.

- I understand your feelings, William, I wanted to go straight to the raw history so you can understand the situation.

understand the situation, there is much more to know but you will learn it with the days in your stay here, although these lands are considered out of the conflict, nothing and no one is out of this conflict in these days, now if you allow me I am sorry that the conversation has been so short but I must leave urgently.

He shook my hand again and rushed back into a room, the agent next to me looked me in the eyes as if he understood my pain for the lands I was leaving behind, it was a before and after, I could not believe that all this was happening.

We returned to my boat where I had many things to tell the group, Butler was not there, I gathered everyone and told them the situation and how little I understood of everything I had experienced in President Fhael's office, the group was more stunned than me, they began to question me that I should have asked this or that, but with a confused mind immersed in the darkness of the story told it becomes difficult to even breathe, we were all in a crisis of not having anything clear, I began to ask where Butler had gone, they told me that he had left the boat as soon as I left with the agent, we do not know where he was going, again we lost Butler but now in unknown lands.

We were silent, pensive, all this was going around in my head, the old humanity, the death of all of us intentionally, who could carry out all these macabre plans and with what intention? When all this came to my mind a deafening sound suddenly invaded from the skies, and an explosion made us lie on the ground, the earth shook and the water shook our ship as if it were made of paper, everything exploded around us, our eyes were wide open and we did not understand what was happening, we ran to the deck and saw the worst war landscape that anyone could observe, not even in our times of war we lived something similar, everything was destroyed, people screamed in the streets, an alarm sound was activated who knows where, but it was heard throughout the city, a voice tried to calm people down, but it was too late, they had reached the Ancestral Republic.

CHAPTER VI - ANAKIM, THE GIANTS OF THE SOUTH

Stunned by what had happened and still not fully understanding the dramatic situation that was taking place in these lands, many images crossed my mind, surely derived from the fear and helplessness of seeing the suffering of my new brothers before my eyes, there were people on the ground under the dust and rubble, like the tragically famous Sodom and Gomorrah, "enemy crossfire" could be heard in the distance, I saw innocent people die that day, everything was getting out of control in just a few moments, we watched the sky full of small silver spheres with red lights that followed the whole scene, I was not sure if they were from the Republic or enemies, but there they were without missing anything of the gloomy scene.

We ran trying to help those we were crossing on the way, but the reality is that we had to leave the boat as soon as possible, we were all going in different directions, the voice that before tried to calm us down, now gave orders that were almost pleas to go urgently to the building of the "Presidential Office Renacer", that's what we did those who were left standing in the middle of a rain of debris and some detonations.

Anguish and anger fell on me like lightning in the ocean, I raised my eyes to the sky begging for some kind of mercy, the sky was in a furious red tone, I could observe that the sun's glow did not burn my sight, it had a dark tone and what I thought was the Moon, stood out in the distance in a totally black color, as in the middle of an Eclipse. I thought then that it was the strangest sky that anyone from the "Known Lands" had ever witnessed, added the strange spheres that danced in the air in all directions, they were like silver eyes observing everything, the next question resounded inside me immediately after:

Who was controlling these small objects, and what was their function? As far as I could see in the midst of it all, none of them were performing any attack maneuvers.

The situation at the time was really heartbreaking, the building was intact and I could enter without major problems, although for obvious reasons there had been some turmoil at the entrance, anyway and despite the existing fear, people respected each other in an extraordinary way, I can not even imagine the chaos that could mean a similar situation in my homeland.

I had lost the whole group in desperation under enemy fire, I felt concerned for the others and with the responsibility by experience in the Continental Navy to put myself at their disposal to help in some way to the city that had just received us in the best way and now suffered the onslaught of an enemy still invisible.

The wounded numbered in the thousands, there were so many equipped rooms that in the face of such an attack of dimensions never seen in my humble wartime past, I was shocked.

I tried to find the team but it was impossible, I could not even recognize one of them, the people who were there in the different corners of this huge building looked at me with some suspicion, I was a "newcomer" from other lands and with me had also come a fierce and fatal attack that would leave at least a quarter of the city destroyed.

I tried to go through the different floors without getting lost and to find the Office of President Fhael, I needed to talk urgently with a high command, I wanted to satisfy my many questions about the enemy, I wanted to put myself at his orders, this attack was not going to be one like any other, it had touched my heart so much that I felt equally part of these lands, as much as the others who suffered at my side, as if my blood had been born here long ago.

To my surprise I found Fhael with a face of extreme concern with Captain Butler, I called his name without being able to wait to arrive among so many people around, Butler performed a kind of typical military salute from afar, without losing customs, I was glad to see a familiar face and it generated me confidence among so much atypical War madness.

I saluted Fhael as best I could, with a faltering voice, who said everything with his melancholic look, he showed to be depressed by the situation, which was not for less.

I put myself under his orders to help in what he needed and required such a situation, Fhael thanked the gesture but commented that nothing we could do but wait for the moment, although in a failed way I tried again to deposit my many questions, the moment deserved it in my mind but Fhael was in a heated conversation in a kind of tiny communicator, where the other voice repeated constantly and the following was clearly heard:

"We are requesting support from the Anakim, we have no choice Fhael, this was a planned attack to destroy a civilian and secure area, there is no turning back."

Butler turned back to me with the typical look of leadership reinforcing my idea that what I had heard, are they talking about what I imagine? I asked Butler lowly, he nodded his head, they are the "Giant Warriors of the South", William.

Fhael heard him and blurted out a sentence that left me even more intrigued:

"Not only that, they are the saviors of our people, the ones who led us to these lands before the reset of our time" he then commented to Butler that he should leave but to do what was needed, and quickly returned to his office with three agents following him.

Butler asked me to follow him and so I did as best I could among thousands of agents coming and going, another attack was feared, war was brewing on the very land we had only set foot on a few hours before.

The captain told me that it was time to rest before embarking on a new journey and another destination, I stared at him as if expressing my fear again, besides I was not sure if our ship was still standing, I could hear explosions outside, it was then when I thought to ask: Where would this destination be and the reason for it, was it something that Fhael had requested?

He explained to me that it was not exactly Fhael's plan but that the moment required it, he would go to look for the team first to gather them here, and once they were all here, we would undertake a unique trip to the Anakim Lands, but first we would pass by their home, I was stunned trying to digest these words, I wanted to have said so many things but my voice barely made a sound that made no sense in any language, Butler then clarified in case it was necessary before my desperate way of expressing myself:

"I'm sorry I couldn't tell you sooner, William, I am as much a part of these lands as anyone else you see suffering here, I was born with the ancestral blood and I am watching my brothers die, apparently they want to repeat history even in these Lands, it is time to save again the only humanity that has survived a Custodial reset, and who can save us all, who better than the very ones who helped cross the Ice Walls back then?", Butler then marched off and got lost among the agents waiting outside.

I lay down on the most comfortable bed my body had ever been in, intending to sleep but who was going to sleep after all I had been through? How would my reason process so much information from a human story never told, How could I not see the eyes of my new brothers falling in pain and not feel that we were on the right side, and that we had escaped from a sinister place that I used to call home, these feelings hit my chest with a resentment and deep venom, I would want at that moment to open the doors to the innocents we were leaving behind, to the loved ones of the Known Lands.

CHAPTER VII – THE DISEASE OF THE HUMAN BEING

I had been able to fall asleep after several failed attempts, among so many thoughts and explosions heard in the distance, thinking that maybe none of this was real, it couldn't be happening, it was too much information to process in my confused mind.

I was abruptly awakened by the captain's voice, "William up, it's time to march!" he said in a firm voice, almost like an order, I could barely grasp the situation and again be aware that we were under enemy attack, an enemy I was still almost completely unaware of.

Butler had gathered the whole team together, everyone was safe and it brought my soul back to my body, we embraced each other as the great team we were and for all the situations we had been through, an almost brotherly reunion in an unknown continent where only negative things were happening all around.

We went out to the central corridor that crossed with President Fhael's door, the captain was worried and ordered us to hurry as much as we could, the thousands of people that were crowded in the building were gone, what had happened to them?

I didn't even have time to ask before the boys commented as they passed by, that the "evacuation plan had been activated" one of them with astonishment told me "we saw big trains and thousands of ships overhead carrying many people at incredible speeds, William".

The captain came back to us saying, that is exactly what we are going to do, we will get on one of those ships that has to leave in twelve minutes, hurry up the pace then we will have time to talk about everything that is happening, I know you have so many questions that will be answered as soon as we arrive to safe lands.

We had barely arrived to the supposed safe lands and now again we were looking for other lands, it seemed that we were turning the lands into unsafe, we were arriving and hell was falling around us, I feared that people would think that we were cursed and we were bringing calamity with us.

Practically running through the desolate streets destroyed by the bombs that had fallen, I managed to look at the sky again and those little spheres were gone, but in their place were passing at incredible speeds some big bluish triangles from one side to the other, I could not help stopping for a minute, when the captain noticed my

when the captain noticed my fault, he returned to his pace shouting at me "William, leave the skies for a second, now is not the time, those flying birds are friends, "the Iron Blues" are making the enemy retreat, now please let's get to our destination urgently".

I had no choice and gave in to such a plea, although it was quite hard for me to let pass such a majestic flight of those blue birds, they were flying from one side to the other, they were flying in a magnificent and singular way, I could not believe that they were being directed by someone or something else, they seemed as if they had a mind of their own.

When we arrived at the supposed destination, there were many agents apparently waiting for Butler and therefore for all of us, although they seemed to be relieved to know that the captain was alive then they reproached us for our delay, and that they only had to wait a minute longer, they practically "put us" quickly on a silver platform and it took us to the top, while we were contemplating a contradictory view, between fire, death and desolation to the other side of a modern city with structures never seen before that represented absolute prosperity. In the sky "the Iron Blues" were still battling against these spheres that were already far from the coast, the captain asked if this view did not remind us of the portraits of Nuremberg and Basel, but we all looked at each other without understanding what he was referring to.

As soon as we arrived at the top floor, some agents greeted us with a warm welcome, commenting that we were about to have a unique experience touching the clouds, these ships were not at all like the ones we had in our minds, if we could ever imagine such a thing.

The structure was huge, and they seemed to be made of one piece. There seemed to be routes in the skies, leading two different ones separately there and back.

These supposedly large iron structures were lost in the horizon, from what I was told by the same agent who received us, they connected every point of the big cities, he told me to prepare myself because the first experience of traveling in these great ships was something that would never be forgotten.

A dark blue ship was waiting for us, once inside the opening closed automatically, I sat next to Butler in seats of 4 people, the interior seemed even bigger than it was on the outside, soon to sit down it started up but we could barely hear a faint whistling sound.

Butler and the agents asked us to try to relax, that getting used to these iron giants was going to take some getting used to at first but then we wouldn't notice. As soon as the trip began, one of the boys was the first to collapse with a fainting spell, but he came to quickly.

I felt dizzy and missed Butler's conversations with the agents, I tried to relax and join this frantic trip that seemed to be ejected like a ball from the most powerful English cannon.

At times we would enter long tunnels, and everything would go dark, at those moments I thought I would pass out too but I got around this feeling of temporary nausea and dizziness as best I could and after fifteen or twenty minutes we were all traveling smoothly.

It was time to pay attention to the beautiful landscape of the Ancestral Republic, "Renacer" in the distance was the most modern and prosperous city that not even the great literary minds could have imagined, the surroundings were tinged with various colors due to the large plantations of vegetables, flowers and fruit trees.

The green was predominant, it was a really emotional view that invited to live in this small Eden, in fact according to what I heard there were some nearby islands called "The Islands of Eden" that even provided a greater spectacle, and its name described them perfectly, although I could not afford to miss listening to the interesting conversation of Butler with the others about the war strategies that were developing.

At a moment when his big talk of plans and strategies ended, I knew it was my chance to again satiate my questions, I had as many as the reader will surely have at this point, I didn't know where to start.

Butler beat me to the punch and outlined the next question:

How much did the last air measurement yield, how much damage do we have in the area? One of the agents replied that they were sure they had acted in time, and for this reason the attack was made in the same area where the numbers showed possible poisoning of the air and nearby plantations.

I could no longer bear this conversation that seemed like undecipherable codes to me and to the whole group, so I got up my courage and asked: "Can you explain to us, which poisoning are you talking about?

Butler looked at the group somewhat with compunction, and explained succinctly:

"They poison the air, let's see, how do I explain? The human that is born in their lands, gets sick quickly due to the work that the Custodians do, this disease is usually implanted in the first humans or better said, the babies left from the last reset, or maybe the second generation as well to make sure, but then this is passed from generation to generation automatically, it is also not uncommon for them to poison the air they breathe, which is the most common way, sometimes to continue to ensure future sick generations or simply docility, it is a very cruel race William, I am sorry that you have to find out all this in such an abrupt way, but sooner or later you have to know.

We were all stunned again by such a statement, what do you mean by poisoning our air? And what is this disease? Or what harm does it cause us? - I asked astonished.

"This disease is practically new, it was used in the last reset," clarified the agent who was listening to our conversation, "we are still studying it closely but what we know is that it makes their bodies age rapidly, and that only a small part of their lives are useful and profitable for them to then give way to the next generation quickly, They prefer it this way because the past longevity brought other conflicts, people had more time to analyze the situation in which they found themselves, they modify the human and mold it to their usefulness avoiding any conflict, the idea is always to fulfill the cycle called "natural" of the next reset".

- Does this mean that they shorten our life span?

"That's exactly what I'm saying, we in the Ancestral Republic live three times longer than you because there is no such modification in our bodies, but they tried recently, they want first to shorten our lives to achieve their control."

Butler interrupted with a blueprint he had in his hand and started to ask again about War strategy issues, I could not fully understand the situation, it was all so confusing and it generated such anger in me that it was hard to handle, I think we all thought the same at that moment, the guys were asking each other and analyzing this trying to understand it. The Custodians were shortening our lives and making them miserable, I understood then that there was no freedom of any form in the Known Lands, how could we free our people from this perverse power?

How could we declare war on an enemy of which we were unaware? And what was the human like without this foul control?

The answer was right in front of my eyes, absolute prosperity was below us, in every boy and girl who ran through the fields freely, where their life seemed to be happy and carefree until their old age perhaps at 240 or 250 years old, how wise could an elder of the Republic be then? How free was a child born there? How much evil existed within each one without the cursed Custodial control?

We arrived at the Capital called "The Ark (El Arca)" in the stipulated time, there were no delays there, except for our delay of one or two minutes, the doors opened and we stopped on a platform where everything was covered by a kind of crystal, if the scenery was already inexplicable by then, the reader will understand that I could not add any words for such a description, these are the moments that I regret not having been born or trained as a literary great, but I assure you that that day we lived the best sunset that someone can have in his life.

There were structures never seen before that touched the skies, besides hundreds of flying wheels, they were like two wheels that joined together forming with other material a sphere that could carry one or two passengers on it, something magnificent to see, another incredible detail was that in spite of seeing the biggest, most illuminated and fullest city of all, there was no noise, everything happened in absolute silence.

CHAPTER VIII - HUMAN GREATNESS

The Capital "El Arca" received us, but as things were going so far, it was clearly not going to be a pleasure trip, at least not at the beginning, Butler ordered us to follow him and after saying goodbye to the other officers, we immersed ourselves in this immense luminous and modern city that my mind so lacking in imagination would never have imagined.

We tried not to lose sight of the captain who never looked back but as is his custom as a leader, he expected his faithful companions to follow him without losing track, it was complex to do so because we were enraptured by the environment at every step we took, the whole group was really surprised, people filled the public spaces, restaurants, and vehicles seemed to always collide but never did, their maneuvers were almost perfect.

In the sky big transparent spheres were walking from one side to the other, most of them were occupied by one person, but in some occasions even two were seen driving those strange balloons that floated and crossed the skies.

Even when the news was fast spreading in every part of the Republic, the citizens of "El Arca" were happily strolling around, as if no war had broken out just a few miles away.

Separating from the captain would have left us in big trouble as the language they used in the capital was not English nor any language I could decipher, another question was already adding to my mind, would this be a native language? Perhaps the oldest one anyone could have heard, from an earlier humanity, and if so, where did it come from?

I sank into my thoughts as I automatically followed the captain, the land of the Anakim, imagining what such a place might be like? A part of me even doubted its existence, it was unbelievable to even imagine the possibility of seeing giants, giants? I asked myself an inner voice. It was even strange to repeat it in my own mind, I think the whole group was in the same situation.

We approached a place that appeared to be a large harbor, many boats were resting, Butler asked us to wait for him while he went over to talk to the officers there.

We took the opportunity to talk to each other, we were all living in a dream that at times turned into a nightmare, from the Eden that could be seen from the heights of the great forests full of colorful flowers to the deadly and bloody roars of these, apparently famous "Custodians" of which we had barely heard until now, and that perhaps I would have liked to never know.

With the experience of a past war and battles at sea that I had under my belt, I could notice that the group was very united and with a lot of strength, I guess that the uncertainty and this knowledge with which we had collided unintentionally, transmitted an immense desire that arose from within us to want to know more and more, we wanted as much information as possible, to unravel this unknown human history in the lands where we were born.

We also began to doubt about the recent attack, was it our fault for escaping from the Known Lands, was this our punishment, were those great walls of ice perhaps artificial, were the Custodians perhaps other humans or were they a race we did not know? Giants, new races, new lands and artificial walls, we began to dig so deep that our theories already bordered on the ridiculous, but everything was already beginning to be unknown then nothing became logical either, our world was changing every second and it had done it forever, like a divine sentence.

Butler approached us and told us that we would take that boat over there (pointing with his hand), it was the boat that stood out the most, similar to the one that approached us as soon as we crossed the Walls, everything was ready to leave for the Anakim Lands, but first, according to Butler, we would have an obligatory stopover in the Captain's lands.

We were able to visit every corner of the luxurious and modern ship, everything was from a different and distant era to the one known to us, difficult to understand, in case it was not already enough to have noticed, that technology was advanced in light years.

They explained to me that we could practically say that these ships handled themselves, besides that we could hardly hear the outside, they were very silent, fast and we could hardly notice the movement in the water, anyway the sea was calm and suddenly this made me realize that the waves were always in this state, their calmest and most neutral form in these lands, at least in all our experience in our trip here. Then that led to another question that added to the immense list that I already had to my credit, did these waters have a totally different way of behaving compared to ours? I was sure of one thing, and that was that the Moon shone at least three times brighter, the color of the Sun was totally different from the known, and there was also another sphere of a bluish-black color, which I noticed when the iron blues battled overhead, at first I imagined that it was part of some technology I did not know, but it was still there, static, in a part of the firmament.

After a few minutes of sailing at truly extraordinary speeds for the whole group, the captain ordered us to prepare to descend, although the situation was tense and certain precautions were taken during the short trip, we breathed a different air as we arrived at this island that had a small and humble port, not so different from those we knew in America, and in the distance many low houses of shiny white color that peeked out from among the green hills.

Butler left his few belongings on the floor and suddenly a little girl who seemed to be no more than six years old ran into his arms, behind him a woman with a pale face smiled as she saw the captain arrive to port, after a deep embrace she introduced us, it was his wife and daughter who welcomed us.

Butler with a cheerful tone confirmed what we all thought, welcome to my land comrades, this is my family and I hope you are comfortable here as long as we can stay.

We settled in some houses adjoining the captain's house, who also invited us to enter and gave us all the comforts, we did not think we would be there long because of the urgency required by the situation in which we were, but Butler said later, it was just over a year since he was at home, and he was not going to waste the time to stay as long as he could with his family.

We stayed two nights on that simple but beautiful island, and during this period I was able to talk to the captain about several points that kept nagging at the back of my mind, that I needed to externalize, I was looking for answers over and over again, my mind would not slow down for a second, Butler knew this and anticipated it as he always did, he was a man who walked several steps ahead of us in every decision and thought.

- "Their minds are somehow modified, to put it in a way you can understand me."

I tried to follow him with my eyes, in an act of inner emptiness, only waiting for him to develop that interesting and disturbing point.

- Butler then went on to say "The ultimate humanity is dependent on your mind, in a totally noxious extreme, you do not detach yourself almost at any time with exceptions, you imagine what exists and what is based on your thoughts, your image created by experiences and through others who also feedback on others thoughts, creating an immense network where each one identifies himself according to where he was born, his status quo or physical condition, but this only does nothing but move away from the true human essence."

"We, those who have blood of ancestral humanity, do not have that permanent attack of the mind with infinite thoughts mostly degrading, and that also mostly are inventions of situations that no longer exist or that will never happen, Humanity in each reset was approaching what the Custodians want from us, because they were modifying both their bodies and minds as the environment, the Lands you left behind is an isolated world, unreal, where evil stands out, wars abound and degradation becomes almost unbearable, but those humans, your brothers and mine too, although from another era, they are not what their minds think every day, that is why history is hidden, because if human greatness were known then nothing could stop us in our growth, because no one would live kneeling if they knew who is tying them with the invisible leash there in that world inside the ice walls.

- I had nothing to say, I remained silent and I kept my words to myself so as not to cry with impotence, I had never heard the captain be so clear, his gaze was lost in the horizon, I kept that night as one of the many unforgettable nights I would have in these glorious and revealing lands.

I asked some other important questions that you will soon understand from the story of what will happen, the next morning when that strange sun would shine again, it would find us sailing towards the lands of the "Anakim".

CHAPTER IX - THE ORIGIN OF THE HUMAN BEING AND THE REVEALING BOOK OF SHE-KI ABOUT THE OTHER WORLDS

The journey to the shifting islands of Thoth went without major inconvenience, the only strange and remarkable thing was that there was no night, the day faded barely on the horizon, but the first night a full and clear Moon appeared in the firmament, and we barely noticed the transition, like an eternal sunset of fire in the distance.

I saw two iron blues pass across the sky at different parts of the last day's journey to the islands of the giants.

It was hard to fall asleep because of everything that had been going on in our lives and around us, we were all waiting for the big moment of contacting giants, it was something we could not even imagine.

We finally arrived at a fairly modern port, perhaps with fewer structures of the majestic in the Capital of the Ancestral Republic, but their ships differed quite a lot from those I had seen before, a certain decline towards military ships stood out, some even seemed to have weapons that I had never seen on top.

As soon as we descended, a man with a very long reddish beard and a woman with a beautiful face and long blond hair welcomed us, first they spoke with the captain and then introduced us to everyone.

Although they were tall, they were no more than 2 and a half meters tall, it was enough to pass us by several long feet.

Stupefied to step on the ground of giants we shook their hands and followed them, the city was not so silent, and that was more like a rural area.

The language they spoke there was also unintelligible to our ears, the captain could not speak it either, but the woman who introduced herself as "She-ki" spoke our language, albeit in a very strange way.

language, albeit in a very strange way, but she was fluent and could make herself understood.

We entered the part that seemed to be the center of this village on a remote island in an ocean also hitherto unknown to us. She-Ki invited us in, their houses were domes of different heights, and there were also huge white towers finished with domes on top, in some there were even figures of giants watching everything, I think I would not want to leave this island without going up there at the top to see that majestic view to who knows where.

I noticed that we were already beginning to naturalize situations that until weeks ago were unthinkable and that we would surely faint if we found ourselves in the situation we are in now, in front of the "Giants of Thoth" without having gone through all of the above.

I had in my mind the imagination of barbarian giants, with only some basic clothing that covered them, but the reality is that this advanced race seemed to come out of some story of parallel worlds, their attire was colorful and adjusted to their large bodies, we could see later approaching the central area, that there were thousands of giants of all sizes, but never descended from two meters twenty or two meters thirty, and we have come to see giants as high as four meters.

Butler told us that this race of giants was so important to know our past, since there was in them ancestral human blood and pure Giant blood of the Ancient Lands of Anak. He told us that later they would tell us a little of the history of our race link, how the ancient and pure giants joined with the ancestral humans to bring forth one of the most powerful forces that ever existed in "The Known Lands" to confront the Custodians.

Known as the Great Tartary, which could have changed the course of our history forever, and that in any case marked a before and after generating radical changes in the "Known Lands" as well as in the surrounding worlds.

She-Ki approached where we were with Butler talking about this topic that I was trying to follow closely without missing any detail and making a mental note of the thousands of questions that arose in my mind at each advance. I noticed that the giant had in her hands a huge book that she offered me saying that this would help me to understand much more about the past of our races.

As soon as I opened it I noticed several maps, she marked a special page where our home, "the Known Lands", and its surroundings were specified, below and on the following pages she also detailed what was known about the Lands, their races and history.

Again, when I thought I had seen it all I felt again a fire burning inside me with each page, stupefied my face was hard in expression trying to imagine this new personal discovery.

She-Ki noticed in my expression that I was sinking in information, she told me not to try to digest it all at once, "with time you will understand and assimilate it", she tried to reassure me.

How many lands are there? I went so far as to ask at his expression with a smile understanding my frustration.

"178 known worlds, at least, according to the information we've been able to gather," he commented.

"But that doesn't count all the lands and islands that exist outside of them," Butler then added.

The kind and beautiful Giant-human as she went on to summarize a bit of some key topics as she showed me some of the pages of this wonderful and unique book.

We stopped at the "Anunnaki" lands, there her face changed, the "Anunnaki" race has always behaved in a hostile manner towards humans since the beginning, and he also commented that they were bound by an old treaty with the Custodians.

Would it be the most awaited moment for me? Would it be the culminating moment where I would know the true beginning of human life? The true origin?

I will not get ahead of myself for the moment, I will only say that this conversation, in case the trip itself had not already done so, changed my life completely, I will go on to detail and transcribe this conversation in the next chapter.

CHAPTER X – THE DOMES, THE LEARNING OF THE WORLDS BEYOND THE ICE WALLS

The past of the giants or Giant-Humans was hidden forever, their technology and bones were as sadly hidden and forgotten as the greatness of their history, and new discoveries of giants will be today and, in the future, simply ridiculed, some even intermingled with beasts that never inhabited these lands. The eternal "Known Lands" where their oceans are stained with ancestral blood, which could have changed everything.

The Custodians made a pact, never the human of the new reset could know, that a force was possible to defeat his invisible colonizer, he would not even know this time that there was a force above that controlled his lands and his environment that made him live an empty life, where the messages would be based on his exploitation of all kinds, his degraded spirit, in this chapter we will see the origin of the human being, an essential being with infinite spiritual potential, as well as why the other races are interested in him. Those who want to keep them in an almost unbearable oppression and those who want to make them escape towards their immense spiritual freedom, is this possible?

The previous day had been so important that I had not even fallen into the world of dreams until my body tried to reconcile in a strange night of sky illuminated by that mysterious and huge full moon.

It was so hard to sleep that the whole group stayed up until what we imagined was very late even though we didn't see the Sun peek out before finally getting a wink of sleep.

Conversations obviously revolved around everything that had been happening to us, but especially the little we had been informed had already fallen like a fierce storm overseas, our minds by then were mere vessels in search of survival, the storm was the truth that not only fell on our face and plunged into our interior, but also generated the most gigantic waves that made each of us reel abruptly.

Have they conditioned our minds so much? We repeated to ourselves over and over again.

Is this story real? But how can we doubt this story when we are in the lands behind the ice walls, and living with the same ancient Giant-Humans? I think that from so much analysis we passed out until a few hours later.

Butler woke us up, we came out of these Domes that maintained a strange temperature that seemed to be regulated, it was always cool in there and outside, the heat was sometimes unbearable.

There were fruits of all kinds, we had never even seen or tasted most of them, some vegetation peeping out of the distance also had strange colors that were hard for me to decipher.

She-ki was wearing a very colorful and summery dress, her face was more beautiful in the sunlight, I think several of the group had been enraptured by her mere presence.

After breakfast we were able to have a private chat together with Butler, and She-ki began to tell me other details of the Book and the history of the races.
Yesterday I told you about the so-called Old Treaty, which was

made between parts of the Custodians and the Anunnaki.

- What were they looking for with that treaty? I dared to ask, I think that this question even came from within me driven by the same anxiety to know everything, but it also generated the way to what was going to be without a doubt a unique conversation. She-ki continued her narrative by saying:

"William, first you have to know that the Custodians and Anunnaki have something in common, and that which unites them is that their technology is primarily based on armaments and military development because they are colonizers from birth, when they arrive in a certain "circle" they look for ways to penetrate it to see how they can benefit, study the life found there and if it serves them they could own it or create different agreements for their benefit in its development."

"In fact it is the seed that they implanted in the ancient humans. The Custodians are also known for their advanced ships and for being among the few to know the 178 worlds or circles around the known."

- What's that about the great dome, what does it mean? I asked innocently.

"William, each circle is divided by one or several different Domes depending on what encompasses that circle, this dome is a kind of membrane that divides a system, this information is very advanced for the time where you come from, but I imagine you have heard of the cellular theory, these circles we could roughly compare them to what we call a cell and its plasma membrane."

"This Dome-Membrane, is a wall invisible to our eyes (although some races can make it out) that divides two systems that are similar or may differ in their totality, but have connections in different parts, what we know from the information taken from the Custodians, is that all the circles or worlds that are known have some connection between the inner and outer system, except one, which is considered the most important and which led just to this Old Treaty between Custodians and Anunnaki."

"These races are adept at manipulating environments as they have sufficient technology to do so within the dome of any known world.

These connections between inner and outer worlds are not simple to find, but the races that have managed to get out and those that base their technological advances both in conquest or in their mission to explore, make long journeys with the reason to gather information from other worlds also developed different types of systems to find the way to find these entrances and exits more easily.

There are also portals that connect different lands but that is another subject that you will discover throughout your stay outside your homelands and how much of the technology works here."

"Now, that circle that I was telling you about the 178 known ones was impossible for them to access even using the most advanced Custodial technology and then this became their obsession. These lands where no one could enter, or at least no one could enter and get out of there alive, are the 'Celestial Lands', and as each Custodial attempt was thwarted an agreement was made with the Anunnaki to jointly develop technology that could open the way inside and unveil the mystery of what was there."

"The reason for their obsession was the rumor that in the Celestial Lands would be found the secret that would lead to being able to penetrate "The Great Dome" that divides the known worlds from the outside."

- What do you mean by the "Great Dome"? - the question came from inside me almost without wanting to interrupt but with the anxiety that all this generated in me.

"Of this Great Dome we have very little information that we were able to gather from the Custodians, what we know so far is that it would be a great Dome that envelops the 178 worlds inside, where the theory goes that no way out or in has ever been found and there is no information regarding what lies beyond."

"The Custodians and Anunnaki worked together with their great scientists to carry out a never-before-seen development basing their technology entirely on discovering the impenetrable Celestial Earths, what would be found there? On that question they based their development of their long years to come.

They reached the point where their technology had advanced exponentially, so much so that they were able to pass through the first Dome, but another problem arose, the beings that passed through the first Dome died pulverized almost instantly, they found no answer to this and tried in various ways and with the use of various races, but they all died in the same way."

"Later in their extensive study of such lands they came to the conclusion that within did not exist physical bodies but a conscious energy which they called "The Source" or "The Source of Life". The theory goes that this energy began to perceive the danger of Custodial and Anunnaki technology and acted accordingly to safeguard its environment."

"Then this conscious energy split taking the body of the "Five Masters" who gave life to the Human Being, occupying lands around your home or homelands.

They first started with "Asgard", to the north, a remote place bounded by mountainous areas very difficult to discover, then as they developed, they took lands in Lemuria, Atlantis, and the center of their lands which they called Hyperborea, which in turn had a direct connection to the outside world with Asgard, their land of origin, by means of a connecting portal".

CHAPTER XI - THE GIANT-HUMANS AND THE GREAT TARTARIANS

Nothing mattered around here more than all this information I was receiving from "She-ki", it was incredible just to imagine where I was and that a surviving gladiator, who had also helped our ancestral humanity to survive, was telling me in great detail about the true human history.

She-ki then continued: "These men animated with the vital energy of "The Source" began to increase in numbers as well as in technology, first they based their technology on race development and welfare, although later they came to develop defense weapons, but they never reached the same Custodial level.

One fateful and dark night the Custodians penetrated the Known Lands and found abundant gold and other minerals, in their eagerness they traveled through every point of these lands arriving to discover outside the first Dome between a zone of high mountains, the famous lands of Asgard, and with them they also collided with the humans living there.

This group of Custodians were surprised by light defense weapons that attacked and automatically pulverized the enemy, igniting an alarm to the other lands inhabited by humans, what was feared was really happening and by then the energy of the Celestial Lands that animated bodies of human beings was not prepared to face them.

Moreover, the Custodians outnumbered the humans by 1000 to 1. Then, a few days later, the inevitable happened, humans surrendered to them.

This was the beginning of a great nightmare that would last until the present day, but why didn't they behave as on other worlds where looting as many minerals as they needed was enough to march on?

Simple, they tried to send humans to the Celestial Lands as a test (it was not strange to think so since they had tried it also with other races) and although the human bodies burned as soon as they entered these lands, they noticed how this energy that lived inside them, always went directly to the Celestial Lands, no matter where this body met death.

In this way the Custodians and Anunnaki have been studying the human being since ancient times, all that effort and development to enter these lands now turned to the possibility that through the human as the fundamental vehicle it could be achieved.

But there was a missing connector that was not simple at all, and this was the power to manipulate these souls or energy that left the human bodies, but that was never possible.

At first they performed the ancient and cruel colonization of lands carried out by these beings in a general way, most of the population is annihilated leaving only their newborn babies, then comes the education necessary to give the new colonized the purpose or function that the Custodians desire.

This attempt to use humans to enter such lands led to countless numbers of beings dying senselessly, in fact in past "resets" led to the sacrifice of many humans together to see if they could manipulate this great energy at will, the great and well known blood rituals by past civilizations.

As I was saying. rituals, diseases, catastrophes, they tried everything, but nothing worked, they even tried to resurrect bodies and a lot of different things.

What happened next is not clear, some historians say that they simply continued with the control of humanity to continue trying to enter, and others say that they only continue to do so for fear that humans can defeat them because they see in them a unique and immense potential among the many existing worlds. For this reason they control them with "resets", and then the famous lies in their education, shorten their life, create plagues, diseases and miseries.

But you are so important that they are not going to let you go just like that. Because inside each one of you is "The Source" which is the most important thing and which keeps alive all the other beings in these circles.

The giants saw all this from the outside, they never got involved in these wars, but then in time they decided to help humanity as they realized that if "The Source" fell, probably the 178 circle-environments would fall as well.

(Here again it is not clear whether the Custodians tried to use any race of giants for the same mission of accessing the Celestial Lands, since it is said that they tried all the races they could find among the 178 Worlds).

After a while the Custodians lost interest in the human as they began to believe that this energy or soul that came out of the human bodies and returned to the Celestial Lands were not the same energy or that failing that, if it was the same, they had no way to manipulate it, also the Anunnaki began in a crisis in their environment due to the lack of gold and minerals essential for their development.

What to use then? They began to use the newly reset human to be able to extract the gold from the harsh and deep intraterrestrial darkness. What better way than to make them believe that they were their Gods and that they would have to worship in obedience to what they required.

The period of creation of many of the known Pyramids was carried out at this time, by the humans themselves with the help of Custodial technology, these Pyramids were nothing more than energy generating centers, which served to control the human and

generate catastrophes if they wanted to, they also tried by this means to control souls again in a failed way.

The Anunnaki Pyramids were deliberately spread over the Known Lands and the other lands, it was also another ancient way of colonizing lands, they leave pyramids as a form of warning of colonized lands, a kind of badge for any intruder entering without permission, it was known that they feared that some colonizing race or what would be even worse for them, a race that would liberate the existing colonies could exist and come from outside the known "Great Dome".

The Custodians and Anunnaki began to confront again, now for control of the Known Lands, the human being and specifically the large amount of gold found there.

The giants took advantage of these inconveniences of the Custodians and Anunnaki to be able to enter the lands. Many moved from these same islands, and from other lands such as the "Free Islands" and entered from the north and south of the Walls penetrating the existing domes.

The Walls surrounding the Earths were built by the Custodians in the past so that humans would not have the opportunity to reach the "inner Dome" or "First Dome", since this discovery would expose the falsity of the theory that was preached without discussion, in addition to begin to question several fundamental points of life in the "Known Lands.

The possibility of an Infinite Earth could never reach human minds as this would open up the environment and awaken the thousands of living energies in human bodies that are numb to the knowledge of their past.

Quickly a great army of giants formed in Central Asia and others began to mingle with the humans living there, (possibly the ancient giants knew of "The Source" within each human being) soon these doubled in number, having a great and potent giant-human resistance to the inevitable attack that would come from the Custodians or Anunnaki, when their internal warfare ceased.

They continued to confront each other in battles that took place even in their own lands, thus leaving the control of the Earths as a liberated zone.

These were the boom years of the Great Tartary and the technology based on free energy, the control of the Lands was almost total, even inhabiting every corner of the lands. It is said that some Custodians and Anunnaki saw their pyramids fall without being able to do much since they had to attend their own War, little by little they were losing the control that escaped them like water through their fingers.

CHAPTER XII – GIANT-HUMANS VS CUSTODIANS IN THE KNOWN LANDS

When the Custodians returned triumphant from their War they found their colony totally revolutionized, now there was a power they did not expect between Giants, Giant-Humans and angry Humans revealing themselves for the years of slavery.

These long years of Giant-Humans developing and basing their technology on weapons of war and defense, added to the fact that much Custodial information was plundered and used for this development and scientific knowledge, led to the climax of a race totally forgotten by the Custodians.

When they returned and analyzed the situation, they knew they could not carry on another war because of the casualties of the last one and all the expense that had been carried out to defeat the enemy, obviously they wanted to start an immediate "reset" but their Pyramids were destroyed and they had lost a lot of power in the manipulation of the environment.

They thought and analyzed several strategies and waited to see how the conflict with the humans would develop, but fearful of this uncertain future.

Another war was born in the "Known Lands", this time humanity would fight together with the giants against their former colonizer, the fierce battles fought cannot be described because it was really something that generated even fear in many of the other circles, every day that the sun set piles of bodies from both sides were observed lying on the lands that were now only battlefields, there were areas covered by a vast and different vegetation that now was nothing more than sand and dead landscapes.

The Custodians also weakened by their last war with the Anunnaki saw that they lost all control, and even feared that later their lands would also be attacked by a humanity with a thirst for revenge, the opportunity to annihilate the Custodians also left a great peace for the "Heavenly Lands".

Everything was heading towards an imminent victory, but something happened in the middle, and this was never achieved,

The Custodians had no choice but to return to Anunnaki lands in order to reach a new agreement with them, there was not much army left that could resist another war but technology and the union was immediately taken in exchange for gold, among other things that we do not know but that possibly have to do with the growth of humanity and the fear of future retaliation".

- Here it is worth clarifying that when the Custodians had to leave to unify against the Anunnaki, they left in command an inferior race called "Greys" of Zeta Reticuli and Orion, they were used to control the Earths while they were gone, but according to the story the "Greys" did not agree with the Old Treaty and the manipulation received, then they were unconcerned thinking that the human being would never rebel or grow in this way, much less imagined a union with a race of forgotten giants.

"These accepted as they also feared losing their lands at the end of the war, even to the Giant-Humans who now had a large army and sought to free themselves from the Custodial yoke in the Known Lands.

The inevitable happened, an unprecedented war took place in the center of those lands, the two forces used all their potential and technology that they immediately put to the test, the Giant-Humans or rather the Great Tartary of free energy also possessed their own ships, therefore the war took place both on land, water and air.

Unfortunately the giant-human power could not resist throughout the harsh battles and not having control of the environment that the Custodians manipulated, this caused wear and tear and deterioration in the troops as well as "natural" catastrophes that grew out of nowhere in important centers, although as I mentioned before this would mark a before and after in all the surrounding worlds, I knew that if they lost this war they were also somehow condemning future generations for several centuries.

The giants had to escape from the lands since defeat was inevitable, and their death was certain, the Custodians would never forgive the giants for having taken up arms and delivered forbidden knowledge to humans, managing to escape where they had entered, through the North and South passages.

Some humans followed them and also achieved this longed-for escape from the Custodial yoke.

The ancient souls of Asgard, Lemuria and Atlantis that inhabited human bodies started from scratch in the lands outside the first Dome known as "The Ancestral Republic" and although hurt by a hard defeat they had the hope to grow again and return with new strategies now with two different missions, to liberate the human being and to finish with the Custodians. Human beings began in these new lands to connect with "The Source" and understand their true past and importance."

Butler interrupted saying that he had already talked to one of the leaders there, and that they did not agree to help us, not because they did not want to but because they feared that their entire race might actually disappear as almost happened last time.

I told Butler of my concern for the lands of the Republic and also for the lands we had left behind, he commented that he doubted they wanted to end up with humanity inside the Walls since of all the "resets" to date, this seemed to be the one that had worked best for them, besides the "Greys" were also under their control and in turn helped to control the human in many other ways.

Since there was high mind control, basic and/or fundamental issues were not dealt with or if they were, they were easily found and reported with some mental problem, immediately sending the "culprit" to a psychiatric facility where they were easily and successfully controlled by other human members.

Imagine if you went back there William and wanted to tell everything you experienced here or the information you gathered, if you had time to tell the others, they would not believe you, and would quickly send you to confinement or possibly death itself.

All this that I had heard gave me many answers that I never imagined I would ever hear, but it also generated many other questions, there was so much to process and everything was running very fast, it was frantic, according to Butler we should leave the islands as soon as possible, he did not even know his plan as usual, he kept the strategy until the end.

We gathered the whole team to leave, we were going to leave the lands of Thoth, and leave behind the great She-ki, who had given me the most important part of this puzzle that seemed indecipherable, a master key that opened so many worlds and possibilities, the lost history of the human being was in my hands.

The boys began to ask me about this talk, and also began to look through the book I was carrying with me, Butler also helped me to answer the thousands of questions that arose, including mine, between all of us we tried to make this as logical as possible for our confused minds while the sun went away and a strange night fell on us, one of the strangest in those lands. The sky was tinged with the purest red and generated a fire-like glow, Butler commented that this "fire" is visible if you sail near the Antarctic ring, it looks like a giant bonfire in the distance, it was something we had even perceived before leaving the "Known Lands".

CHAPTER XIII "EL ARCA" - THE PROSPEROUS CAPITAL

After spending that strange night of fire mixed with many theories that we were trying to deduce from She-ki's book, it was a very strange sensation that went from extreme to extreme, to think that we were a point far away from everything and we had come to understand from one minute to another that we were "The Source", that conscious energy of the Celestial Lands that lived in each one of us, and also united us to the ancestral humans and to all those who had lost their lives in each "reset" manipulated and hidden.

We began to spot birds fluttering around our ship, denoting that we were approaching land, although we suspected it we could not confirm it with the captain all the way, but the city that awaited us was again "El Arca", the modern capital of the Ancestral Republic.

The first rain since we arrived in these lands began to fall very slowly, just when I was beginning to think that in these latitudes there was no such phenomenon. The lights of the city were coming on in the distance, this immense city of "El Arca" was an invitation to imagination and confidence that such a perfect and peaceful life could be possible also in the dark environment between the ice walls, without the control of the Custodians or any intruder race among us.

We also began to understand that simplicity was what made everything else great, stepping on the grass with bare feet, the birds perching in the most modern harbor, the very rain that gave it a tinge of melancholy gray from the sadness of thinking that not all of humanity was going to be able to witness what our eyes were seeing right now.

Even though we had lived through a furious attack and the most devastating we had ever seen, this immense city gave us the assurance that all would be well, that this could never fall, millions of "Ancestors" were living their lives as close to what we once dreamed of as children, what we dreamed of for future generations, a place of peace and love where there is no pain or suffering, where work does not mean exploitation, where there is no dirty politics or wars for territory or power, no discrimination or stereotypes, no social difference, everything is shared and happiness is breathed, welcome to the "Ancestral Republic" was heard in the distance, in their own clear language, according to Butler's translation.

What was Butler's plan now? - we wondered.

The captain commented that we could get lost and investigate by immersing ourselves a little inside the city, remember that nothing could be bought with gold or use money since they used another form of exchange there, he explained. The plan was not clear, but he would

 The plan was not clear, but he would immediately meet with Fhael and other leaders from different important places in the Republic.

The boys got lost in the big city and I was left alone, pensive, amidst a torrential rain that fell on my face, although of calm appearance, dejected inside, I kept sinking in my deep thoughts of a human future that could not be.

How to overcome this shared misfortune? I asked myself again and again.

I still had so much to discover in that great Book of She-ki, would I find any halo of calm in it?

This information received had fallen worse on me than on the rest, I now felt guilty somehow, that I could not do anything to free the millions that were behind, and that in addition we had been persecuted and attacked in these distant lands, What heart resists before such an onslaught? What heart could not suffer for the now distant brothers that still remained within this vile environment?

Many hours had passed and I was walking through the streets of this colorful city, some few people were crossing my path, I felt their understandable strange look, my way of dressing was not suitable for this modernity, I felt like a caveman even worse if I tried to talk to them, so I continued my way only observing.

Would they understand that we were brothers and shared the same suffering? And a myriad of questions crossed my mind at every step and the few people I looked deeply in the eyes.

One man even tried to talk to me but I only managed to wave my hands explaining that I did not understand what he was telling me, I only said "Fhael" as if to answer a name known to all and this man pointed to a large building a few blocks away.

There were not even puddles of water that accumulated, the whole system was perfectly functioning so that it did not generate any flooding, modernity hit my face so many times that it was difficult to interpret, I dare not even mention the drawings that came out of the walls that projected humans interpreting the most beautiful melodies that sweetened the ears of passersby.

I returned to the port somewhat crestfallen, I had everything a person needed in front of my eyes, I was before absolute happiness but the pain of not being able to share it generated an immense sadness in me, I also kept seeing the faces of the people who fell in

"Reborn".

Butler was returning driving a modern vehicle, when he saw me he stopped it and invited me to get in, his face transmitted some joy, then he commented to me:

- William, we have not been able to get the Anakim to help us directly, it is understandable you know, they do not want to risk their entire race again, but I know that they will help us in the long run, we have won this battle and we do not believe that the Custodians will attack these lands again for a long time, we gave them a lesson that our technology is still more alive than ever, they tested us and I assure you that they came back with fear.

Then he continued explaining to me, with some questions that I could ask on our way to the port of "El Arca", apparently the Guardians were not aware of the technology that had been developing the "Ancestral Republic" in the last 100 years, in conjunction with the Anakim race, they thought that this attack would make them directly tremble and possibly surrender immediately as happened in ancient times in Asgard and other lands.

This had to be taken advantage of in the following years if we were to have a chance to regain the Known Lands and free the brethren from the last reset, but all should be careful, any move that is not planned in advance could cause another reset and the death of millions.

CHAPTER XIV - THE ARTIFICIAL WALLS

We met in the boat that we used in these last trips between Thoth and "El Arca" and Butler told the group almost the same thing that we had been talking about in the return vehicle, but he put more force to his words and his joy overflowed in every part of his face, he had even got something to toast and the whole group was at its most joyful since we arrived, unfortunately this joy was not penetrating my mind and much less in my heart.

I was still distantly trying to understand what would be the right move to change everything, I kept wondering if this was really possible, and if so, how many years of there within the walls would pass while, I was totally involved in freeing my brothers in there.

Butler tried to cheer me up, it was time to change history and this didn't happen every day, so I hid my temporary disenchantment and joined in the toast.

There was no need to even ask about a possible return to our homelands, this was ruled out by absolute, somehow in the toast I closed my eyes with prayers towards the loved ones I feared I would not be able to see again, can a prosperous place like this be enjoyed if not shared with loved ones?

Butler knew inwardly, he went ahead to tell us that we would soon be visiting the Known Lands again and that we could help much more on this side than by entering there and becoming an easy custodial prey.

They would never forgive such a "betrayal" of escaping from their nets and on top of that recovering a large part of history that was never told, and we, the whole group, did not care what they really thought either but it was our duty to take care of ourselves and stay away for the time being and plan our next visit.

Butler brought us a lot of information on how the Republic worked, he also gave us several books, among them many on the language spoken there. As in "Renacer" and elsewhere English was spoken to perfection, there were several books with translations of the arcane language to English and vice versa, as the captain said, it was time to start studying.

Several years had passed, among so many things I learned during my stay was that time passed slower in these lands compared to the Known Lands, it was undoubtedly what I had more trouble understanding, there was a whole library on time, perception and sense of the passage of time.

As an experienced person with a background in major battles in the U.S. naval force, I eventually gained Fhael's trust, and by unanimous decision I became the naval Commander-in-Chief of the "Ancestral Republic", from there I was able to study more about the defense of the Republic, its technology and its development along with the vision for the future.

We carried out projects of possible attacks on the Known Lands without affecting civilian life, but the missions were almost always discarded due to the difficulty I had in finding the real bases of the Custodians, since they moved from one place to another using portals and also almost never had long stays in the Lands but returned to theirs always leaving some leader guarding.

It was really easy for them with the implementation of the ice walls the human possibility of even reaching the first Dome was almost impossible, besides the conditioning that existed by the media and the academy, they had really created humans that would repeat to exhaustion what their books said, and would even guard the walls until death without knowing that they really existed behind them, only by order of their superiors.

The creation of paper money was also key for everything to work according to his master plan, now everything was given so that the humanity of the Known Lands would never know their true origin nor the lands that were waiting for them behind those frozen curtains.

Can you imagine any possibility that the human with the little technology that existed could navigate between giant blocks of ice, find even a passage and not even know if that passage would give him the possibility of crossing that Dome?

The possibilities were clearly reduced to one in a million, but we had succeeded and they were aware of it, so it would not be strange to think that they would use the human militia to guard their own brothers, most of them out of ignorance and others for royalties.

The bases in the Antarctic ring and the exclusion zones would not take long to arrive, as Butler predicted some time ago, it was known that other security measures would be taken because of the past war and the defeat in "Reborn" would bring consequences.

CHAPTER XV - MANIPULATION IN THE KNOWN LANDS

In all this time that has passed I became more and more an arcane ancestral, I did not handle the language to perfection, but I made myself understood, I was interested in science and technology, I tried to learn as much as I could from those minds really advanced and specialized in the matter.

I learned a lot about how our body works in as much detail as I could, the bacteria that lived in us and what was different from a real disease to one created by laboratory, they were more surprised than me when the group made us different analysis to see everything we transported from our homelands, there were so many bacteria and viruses that had been modified and created for different purposes by the Custodians that it was difficult to count, in fact it was known that their plan was still going on every year to continue creating new ones.

They had people infiltrating the lands who passed information every so often, with Butler and the attack on "Reborn" they stopped sending men for quite a while, and neither did the infiltrators come back to make sure they could not be discovered working there, the whole operation would fall apart and we needed as much information from in there as possible, we had to be one step ahead of them or else we would never have a chance to win.

I was getting used to the fact that there was no social difference, we all lived relatively the same way and no one lacked the basics to have a full life.

The President of the Republic and the group of leaders, although they lived in a remote rural area, by their own decision, did not have any luxury, nor did they receive a different salary from the rest, anyone had a voice in politics (if you can call it that, since it differed significantly from the known) and their ideas were listened to. There was no crime at all and, for obvious reasons, no penitentiary.

Respect for the life of others was the main motto and everyone voluntarily adapted to it, it was something natural that was breathed every day. Spirituality and introspection were fundamental and were taught from childhood, they were part of the education, first going through spiritual growth and then moving on to the rest.

They tried not to have an image of themselves, since the mind could deceive them imagining that they were something or someone for others when in reality they would be based on the subjectivity of others, not having an image and not living from the past were pillars that I struggled to understand for years, two fundamental pieces of a puzzle destined for such growth, they called it "the death of the ego".

From there they based any knowledge and learning that would come later, never the other way around, first to know oneself and then to know the world around them.

They taught me a lot about the great masters who had visited our Earths and who were still remembered, the messages they tried to deliver based on what was written before, but all those messages had been distorted or intermingled with dirty business by the Custodial sector, they would never let spiritual growth become present in each one, besides mixing it with dirty money they would also infiltrate several people who would confuse spiritual growth with religious themes to confront sectors or simply false prophets who predicted future chaos.

The few periods of growth that existed within the walls of ice went hand in hand with moments of peace, without great warlike conflicts, but sooner or later some great war would come, or attacks, plagues, pandemics, always elaborated from some sector (always from the same radicalized power) that would interrupt human progress with possible spiritual growth and this was not going to stop.

Politics was also implemented in conjunction with various societies that led in the control of these limits manufactured from the beginning and that would be modified according to the many wars that existed until today, the so-called countries were just another form of control, where there were supposed "leaders" who ruled but in reality were easily adapted to the same custodial power.

This hierarchical form of control based on the paper money system would be key to absolute control in the development of this new humanity, science would then enter its key role where it would drag society to an extreme spiritual emptying basing its life on mere material facts.

People would then seek to increase their collection of colored paper and would turn away from love for their surroundings, even for themselves, their image would be transformed and reduced forever into simple biological functions. What would then be the dream of a profoundly sick society?

The real battle would then be found internally in each of the humans of the Known Lands, but their realities would be distorted always imagining that the central problem is the other's, hate would win over love by the time humans would notice it would already be too late.

The road to a great dictatorship would seem inevitable, the true feelings of love and spiritual growth as a whole would be less and less valued, and without this we could do little from here, since they would take us as bitter enemies and would join the Custodians without knowing it to annihilate us, their military forces work together when only a minority knows it, the great positions and not all of them.

The system was in place and only details were left for the human alone, without even knowing it, to walk the path that the Custodial power had drawn in his destiny. Then the humans would only take care of this system, the lack of spiritual growth added to the real value given to the material and the system based on paper money was all that a society needed to fall into the vile plan and defend it to death.

CHAPTER XVI – THE PLAN TO FREE THE HUMAN BEING

While there was a direct plan to free the humans who were still trapped under the Custodial yoke and manipulated since birth by the lie, it was very risky as it could put at risk not only the millions who lived within the Walls but also the ancestral humans of the Republic and races of the surrounding lands.

Butler arrived one morning to my office together with Fhael, and they told me that they had devised an alternative that could be effective, the Custodians were strong in weapons and war strategies, they based their whole life on that development but they had weaknesses like any race, and this could be found in the depth of their intelligence, not to be misunderstood, they were extremely intelligent beings and great caretakers of their colonies, especially the human, who would be the only being which they never released after several long "resets" throughout history, but they found weak points where they could attack.

Their fear could still be felt from a distance, they were not happy that ancestral humans and Anakim still existed around their most important colony, but they had not tried to attack our lands in these many years that had passed, that put us ahead, if they detested us, they had enough technology and military force to try to destroy us, what had led them not to make more attacks?

The meeting with Fhael and Butler lasted more than four hours, they had developed a series of different plans that supplanted the previous one in case of failure, all were based on attacking what was considered the weakness of the enemy, this was precisely their little or no spiritual development.

Another great discovery was their radar system near the entrances to the Known Lands penetrating the Dome, when an "ancestral" entered through the known passages, small and even some large earthquakes were generated in surrounding areas. It was an extreme surveillance system that put them on alert and sent support forces, for that reason it is quite common that the earthquakes were almost always in the same area, and is also the answer to why we were not sending more people for a long time, and we tried that those who were there did not return to continue collecting as much information as possible from day to day in the manipulated environment.

The important thing then was to find another entrance or create one (this was so far impossible, we had not been able to enter by force in any Dome, and it was unknown if this could really be done) nor could we use any portal since all of them were controlled by the Custodians, but the exhaustive study of the closed zone in the external part of the same added to that everything that was proposed in the Republic really was carried out, made that was created through safe ice melting based on statistics not to generate floods, an area called "Summer Portal" (apparently with technology of the ancient Anakim) where entry was possible but could not yet be confirmed if by then the sophisticated control did not cover that area.

If possible, we could then send different "ancestors" into the lands and subtly use their means to infiltrate important information, the Ancestral Republic, the possibility of other lands, and the real human past would be mentioned as much as possible, sometimes it did not matter so much the name by which our lands were known, The important thing was to know about the lands behind the ice walls, as long as it did not alter the day to day life as it would raise great suspicion, many people who carried out these missions were locked up in different institutions, so we were very careful in spreading the information.

We knew that the great part of humanity would not even pay attention to these facts due to the existing conditioning of several generations which would lead to not really pay attention, and although a priori this would seem something negative, in reality it helped us since we gained time in being able to carry out the other plans, until all would finally unite in a single plan or mission, but for that they had to work in parallel and it was an arduous task to carry out.

The plans were really excellent since they did not cause any harm to the human being, to reach the necessary critical mass was going to be complex anyway, for that reason there was another alternative that consisted in carrying out a very deep spiritual teaching, trying to break the human conditioning within the vile environment.

When the human being develops through different techniques implemented by the ancestors in the Known Lands and can block as much as possible the conditioning and therefore the mind manipulated by the Custodial control, then it was going to be easier for many to open up to the possibility that another reality existed outside the ice walls.

These great ice walls would sooner or later become visible and genuine human expeditions would also collide with them, but it was well known from our lands that any idea of going beyond would surely be blocked by generating fear, or directly by force through what they always use, military intervention.

CHAPTER XVII - THE SUMMER GATE AND THE SPIRITUAL EDUCATION

The "Summer Gate" was a success since the Custodians were not noticing our presence when entering the Lands for several years, the whole group and even Butler were forbidden to enter by order of Fhael who considered that if they found us there, not only would they put an end to our lives but they would try to get information from us using any means, and the whole plan would run a serious risk, as we said the plan had to be perfect or not exist at all, because a failed plan was an assured reset.

The years went by and the plan of the spiritual awakening of the human being in the Known Lands had been increasing and was developing in a correct and safe way.

The teachers who entered through the mentioned "Portal" were able to carry out the teachings and the form of education that any child received here in these lands, prioritizing the importance of the human soul, unconditional love and empathy.

Unfortunately, as we imagine, certain black hands began to be noticed around these teachings, confusing the human being and causing many to move away, these three great premises began to be corrupted as well as to become a cruel business.

But as I said before, there were other plans to supplant these others when things began to get dark, it was a constant struggle so that our incidence would not be discovered, but neither should we let the plans fall into the hands of the custodians completely.

It was time now to carry out another plan that would bring consequences, a navigator and faithful friend would arrive from these lands with a vessel built here simulating the time of that moment, and would tell his story to the world, he would reveal major issues that needed to be known for those who wanted to listen, Antarctic passage between walls of ice, discovery of other lands, the Ancestral Republic would be named for the first time in the history of this humanity (with different name), the story would be intermingled with themes of the time both economic and social for its apprehension, we knew the system created based on the strong scientific conditioning by means of heliocentrism, it was no easy task.

The ancestral navigator spent some time in a well-known harbor within the ice walls, where he showed the curious a lot of real information about the Republic and the human past, including about the Giant-Humans.

Before the story was published, a lot of information was manipulated, and the story came out half-baked being quite confusing and leaving several important points unmentioned, the author ended up disappearing and being locked up.

My faithful friend returned urgently to the lands as this would draw the attention of the Custodians who would seek by all means to understand how the information had been leaked.

While they were confident in their manipulation they would seek other means to dissuade him, and we knew that a not so friendly visit was expected that could come from either the Known Lands, Custodial or Anunnaki.

The Custodians avoided us again, and this made us stronger, the

Giant-Humans as Butler once remarked, would sooner or later give their help, and great technology was again shared, and with this we were again ahead of the custodial advance.

What were the moves of the Custodians in this "Silent War"? They would use the human being to match their technology, this would bring great consequences as the human being was not prepared for the use of such advanced technology coupled with custodial colonizing conditioning, it was a time bomb that was not long in coming, great wars and a deadly plague were precipitated into the environment for the enjoyment of the Custodians.

Human expeditions to Antarctica began, financed by leaders who had direct connection with the reigning power, they knew they had to focus on education to continue corrupting the new human generations, several "space" achievements would come to lay solid foundations of heliocentrism.

The possibility of other lands behind the Ice Walls would be almost buried, they started then with the creation of bases around the entire Antarctic ring added to the exclusion zones, a strong militarization of key areas. Also not long after the "Summer Gate" was discovered, the Custodians took this as a game to demonstrate their power against ours, we feel that in a way they enjoyed it but they also knew they were risking too much.

A few years before the first custodial attack on our lands called "Operation HighJump", by means of a large number of human soldiers and custodial technology, the media barely mentioned it, but it was one of the biggest moves made by any military force.

largest movement by any military force in the history of the "new humanity".

The leader was known as "Richard Byrd" and was used in several missions in reconnaissance of other lands, but in the official missions he would never reach our lands, although his attack could endanger our people, both us and the Anakim had no intention of attacking them but to make them withdraw their armed forces in a peaceful way, the Anakim masters talked several times with their leader, but another force entered the conflict and a great battle was fought just behind the first Dome.

Then the same leader would make contact several times with the Anakim masters and would also help us to carry out the plan of human awakening within the Known Lands becoming an infiltrator for a while, eventually by choice or obligation this changed dramatically and as we were informed the military leader delivered valuable and secret information of the Anakim technology, and was the first of the group of the "new humanity" to be sent to Mars in recognition of his work.

Attacking us with other human beings was one of the many perverse strategies of the enemy, it was their way to demonstrate their power and make us face our past, since we sought to liberate it and not to confront them in absurd battles that were defended by mere conditioning.

We knew that all this game that they were carrying out would end abruptly by their way of acting, we were going to continue gaining ground in this awakening, and they would start attacks within the environment with the different techniques as always, natural disasters, pandemics, wars between nations, etc.

Those academic books that until now seemed untouchable began to be strongly questioned and the entire academy began to reel from the possibility of another model. The Infinite Earth would begin to emerge and would be the ultimate plan that would give way to the final liberation attempt.

CHAPTER XVIII – OSIRIS AND THE INDEPENDENT LANDS

What did we need to accomplish our last step?

That our brothers change their perspective and break the conditioning was key, our forces could never liberate a people who defended their oppressor, in their minds we would be the colonizers who put at risk their current state and also their lives.

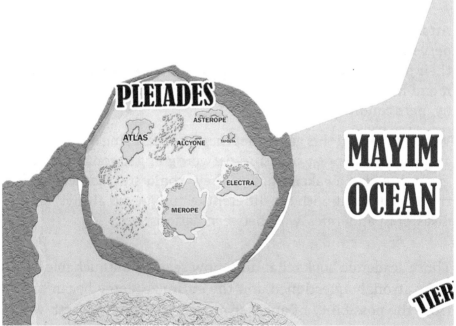

The custodial system was strongly implanted, the existing air pollution also hindered our mission. Although there was great resistance from several sectors, it was still not enough for us to act.

Surprisingly, several other races visited us with the intention of acting against the custodial yoke that was really exhausting as well as threatening their "Circles", all help was welcome, the "Pleiadians" were interested in also being able to liberate "The Source" and annihilate the oppressive races.

Their system was close to the second dome existing near the "Mountain Walls" and the passage between the "Mermaid Lands" and the "Island of Death" was unfeasible, not many could survive the beasts that existed there, so everything had to be done by air.

The Pleiadians had been under Custodial power for some time and had left them on the verge of extinction, their great technological development of ships and spiritual made them miraculously resist and today they became a great free society.

Being close to the Celestial Lands they were also aware of some of the Custodial attempts to enter, they have seen how they used humans on several occasions as well as other races.
In the "Lands of Mars" there were several colonies of different races that had been moved by the Custodians and Anunnaki.

the Custodians and the Anunnaki, they wanted to populate the place with several races where they were in control.

The local race was undeveloped and had not put up much resistance in their colonization.

The humans that were there now all belonged to the "new humanity" of the last reset, and all of them had "earned their passage" by the help given in different missions against their own brethren, we had labeled these lands as noxious in reference to the future.

The lands that were outside of any circle were really disregarded by the colonizers, as they considered that most of them did not have any mineral or race that could be of interest to the Custodians or Anunnaki, in fact many lands had been overlooked in their travels, observing them very overlooked.

This had generated that many races would begin to develop in these lands, as they were for a long time prosperous places without the intervention of colonizing races.

Then in the period of the creation of the great Pyramids and the exploitation in Egypt and Central America, some humans were sent to the Lands behind the Dome, together with Custodial leaders, but they never revealed any passage but were transferred with the use of hallucinogens and in altered states of consciousness, many of which were presented to them as different types of Gods.

The immense land of Osiris was the beginning of the end of the peace of the lands surrounding the great Wall of Mountains, along with the thousands of archipelagos in the deepest ocean known.

Osiris, one of the Custodial leader took a colony of humans to these lands, but they never let these humans manage to leave, they did not want them to ever discover important lands like Lemuria or Atlantis since at that time there were still vestiges of human birth and their great advance that had been left there.

CHAPTER XIX – THE LANDS OF ORION AND THE GREYS

These lands were inhabited by the race known as "Greys".

known as "Greys", these beings were hostile and also based their technology on weapons of destruction for attack and defense, oriented to colonize, although no circle was known to be colonized by them, some lands near other "orien-worlds" were taken by this central power.

Together with their neighboring lands of Zeta Reticuli, this race had been colonized since almost their beginnings by the Anunnaki, who had used them in several expeditions and missions to other worlds in the reconnaissance of the "Terra-Infinita".

As we commented they also fulfilled functions in the Known Earths and then in the Earths of Mars, who also had a colony helping the Custodians in their experiment.

After they had failed in their mission to control the human (in the period of growth of the Great Tartary) where they had also lost valuable information of all the circles that integrated this "Great Dome", some battles were fought between Greys and the Custodians, this also ended up helping the human being as well as the Anakim prior to the reunion of the Custodians with the ancient Anunnaki.

There is a theory that these beings had been a direct creation of the Anunnaki as an inferior race that could serve them for different purposes, since they used cloning as a direct form of subsistence and were very robotic in their functions and movements, in fact these beings are completely devoid of emotions.

But the reality is that they were born inside the Dome known as "Lands of Orion", and with similarity to the race of Zeta Reticuli, after the confrontation with the Custodians they had been close to total disappearance, having to resort to their great scientific advance and base their survival on the cloning of beings.

CHAPTER XX – THE LANDS OF MARS AND THEIR LOST CIVILIZATION

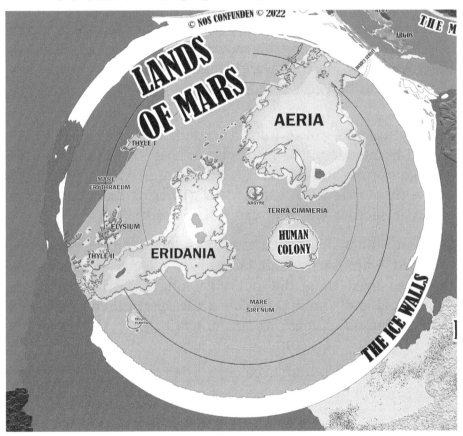

These lands harbored a great variety of life, the vegetation was abundant and it is the Circle with the greatest variety of animals, flora and fauna known.

Its lands were considered one of the most fertile, and it was the first Dome where the Anunnaki were able to penetrate and colonize.

The original beings of Mars at the time of colliding with these beings, resisted as best they could but it would have been lethal.

They were very proud beings and great defenders of life and their lands, they all perished in battle, the last beings committed suicide when they saw that they were going to be part of a great colonizing race, knowing this sad story their loss is regretted since the true and real Martians were beings that based their technology on purely spiritual growth.

The Anunnaki began to inhabit these lands and use them as a second home due to the proximity to their own, then with the passage of time and the treaty with the Custodians, they began to use this Circle as an experiment gathering many races from different colonies, which we can still find today.

The first humans sent there settled in "Aeria", an immense area provided with fertile land but the conflict with other races that also lived there did not take long to arrive, while the Custodians and Anunnaki enjoyed the spectacle, on Mars took place "Dantesque scenes" in wars for territory.

As time went by, the human colony settled on another island close to the Lands of "Aeria" because they lost territory.

Of the "last humanity" the first human to visit them was Richard Byrd in one of his expeditions crossing the South Pole, obviously commanded and helped by his Custodial leader "Nimrod", several soldiers of the U.S. Navy and some invited leaders of secret societies (some of them famous politicians) managed to cross the passage that is known today with his name.

In the central lands of "Argyre" there is a portal with a direct connection to the Anunnaki Lands established there at the beginning of colonization.

Today it is a prosperous area and there are no major conflicts, in fact it is a land that some humans can visit as a reward for tasks performed for The Custodians. It is known that some of them even stay there because they manage to rejuvenate their bodies and get to live long years compared to the Known Lands and the toxins existing in the polluted air they breathe.

CHAPTER XXI – THE LAST GREAT PLAN

I was sitting on the shores of the beautiful capital "El Arca", pensive, my body had begun to feel very strange a few weeks ago, the sea covered my feet and my gaze was lost in the horizon. There where I found my lands of origin that I never forgot and that will always be inside me, together with my memory were the faces of my loved ones, many had already disembodied a long time ago.

I made sure they knew my true destiny and my gifts were delivered safely, otherwise they would have surely imagined that I had died overseas in my madness and obsession for a journey with an uncertain destination, my body in those lands would have easily passed the hundred years and I was like a man in my fifties, however something was not right.

What would be my destiny now, would I die in these beautiful lands of the Republic?

The Sun was falling and with it another day without liberating that paradise turned into a prison called Earth, how many people had to die waiting? Without even knowing it, in their suffering day by day, where disenchantment was as possible as perverse wars and false power.

I sat on the cold sand and my body felt as thousands of piercing needles went in and out of every pore of my skin, I was facing a pain so deep that my body gave way, lying now looking madly at the projection we called firmament, with the faithful companions of every navigator, the stars also observed my loneliness, many members of the group had already left prematurely due to our damned contamination, our sick bodies were regenerating very slowly in these lands and we were only a few survivors of the new humanity crossing the "Ice Walls".

I felt privileged to spend my days here but the pain was permanent, something that did not let me enjoy knowing that many brothers were dying in there without being able to perceive the true love that we carried inside.

Thousands of "Ancestors" were still sacrificing themselves by entering between the Walls to hell itself, knowing that the contaminated environment or the Custodians themselves would kill them sooner or later, everything was based on the liberation plan, which with successes and failures was carried out and was still being tried, we had won so many battles in there without any weapon but thought, love and the spreading of the idea of inner knowledge, what every human carries inside.

We had also made remarkable improvements in the air that was breathed and on the basis of all the laboratory created diseases.

My old friend Butler came over and sat next to me, touching my shoulder, knowing I didn't have much time left, understanding it all he commented:

"William, hold on mate, the time of freedom is approaching, they began to hurry in their desperation, a new pandemic will strike soon, we are entering every day more and more Ancestors to the Known Lands, we will use their own means and when they realize it they will be bent, the new humanity will understand that they are under a dirty and perverse power. We are close to reaching as many humans as we had planned by assuming our responsibility.

The moment will come and then we will make ourselves known, with the help of the Anakim who monitor night and day around the walls, this time cannot fail and if destiny demands it, then we will get as many as possible out of there, resist to see the glory of freeing our brothers, so that the true path of spiritual knowledge begins.

I smiled at such an assertion, I gave him my many notes that I had been writing since I left the United States, I wanted everyone to know the odyssey of that group that went through the most incredible places and saw the most beautiful and hidden landscapes, who knew happiness and true love.

This story will be delivered to my brothers there inside the walls of ice, there were already so many truly interested in the Republic and in these glorious lands of infinite prosperity and this knowledge that it would be the best way to communicate with them.

My body trembled and suddenly silence invaded, I could only see the firmament, the "iron blues" were crossing at full speed, where were our ships headed? Would it be the time to wake up everyone? Were we really ready?

These lands exist, I repeated over and over again inside me, we are guiding you, the battle is real and it is internal, the spiritual growth will free us all, resist, freedom is coming, trust, we are waiting to free you all.

N O S   C O N F U N D E N

YouTube Channel: Nos Confunden

Name: Claudio Nocelli

Instagram: @NosConfunden
Website: https://nosconfunden.com.ar/
Personal Instagram: @eddienosconfunden
Facebook: Nos Confund3n

MAPA TERRA-INFINITA COMPLETE

Author: Nos Confunden (Claudio Nocelli)

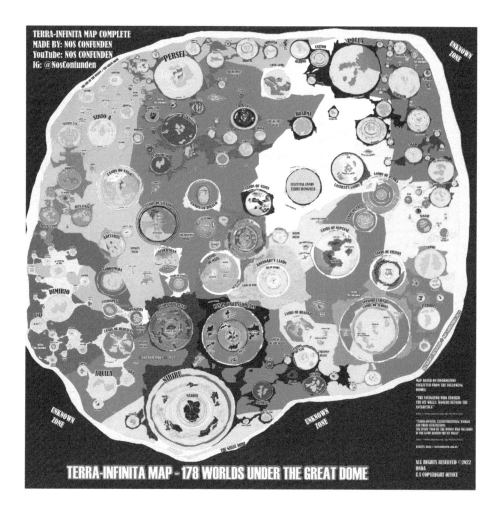

LIBROS DE ESTE AUTOR

Terra-Infinita, Extraterrestrial Worlds And Their Civilizations: The Story Told By The Woman Who Was Born In The Lands Behind The Ice Walls

The story told by the woman who comes from the lands behind the ice walls, in the "Ancestral Republic", daughter of the navigator William Morris, who will provide information that was hidden from us for a long time about the worlds that are crossing the poles and the secrets of extraterrestrial civilizations. We will also be able to discover the human history before the Last Reset and the continuation of what happened to her father when he returned to our lands. This can change everything.

The Lands Of Mars: 178 Worlds Under The Great Dome

178 Worlds Under the Great Dome - Volume 1 - The Collection of the hidden Books about lands beyond the ICE WALLS
The lands of Mars hide much more than we imagine, here we can read the stories of the origin of the Martians in conjunction with the ancestral expeditions of the humans who live behind the Ice Walls.

Chapt. 1 - Where does the information from the Other Worlds come from?
Chapt. 2 - MARS, A Great Zoo
Chapt. 3 - The "Red Planet" Stained with Innocent Blood

Made in the USA
Coppell, TX
10 August 2023

20215756R00059